The Haunted Underwear

by Janet Adele Bloss

cover art by Gabriel
inside illustration by Don Robison

Published by Willowisp Press
801 94th Avenue North, St. Petersburg, Florida 33702

Copyright © 1992 by Willowisp Press,
a division of PAGES, Inc.

Printed in the United States of America

4 6 8 10 9 7 5

ISBN 0-87406-592-5

One

I slid my arm around Star's furry neck. "He's driving me crazy," I whispered into her ear. "I wish we had never adopted him!"

My big collie dog licked my face and wagged her tail. Her chocolate brown eyes looked up at me. I think she understood how I felt.

"He's the worst brother in the world," I moaned. Star licked my ear. Then she chewed her rubber mouse until it squeaked. The mouse was her favorite toy.

"Good old girl," I said, giving her a pat. I was glad that at least one thing hadn't changed. Star was still the best dog a girl could have.

Star lay down beside me with her rubber mouse held gently between her teeth.

I sat in the grass wishing I had someone to talk to. Almost like magic, my best friend Lynn appeared in the distance. She was pedaling her bicycle along the dusty country road.

"Hi, Kelly!" she called, waving her hand. Star barked and ran out to the road to see Lynn. "Hi, Star," said Lynn. "Caught any gophers lately?"

She pedaled her bicycle up my driveway. "Boy!" she exclaimed. "It's two miles from my house to yours. It sure gets hot!" Lynn wiped the sweat from her face. "What time are you leaving for the lake?" she asked. "Maybe my mom will let me go, too. I could borrow one of your bathing suits."

"We're not going," I said gloomily.

"I thought you always went swimming on Saturday," said Lynn. She looked disappointed.

I groaned and brushed an ant from my shoe. "It doesn't look like we'll be going to the lake ever again," I said.

"Why not?"

"Mom says she thinks Stevie's afraid of water," I answered, sighing.

Lynn plopped down on the ground beside me. "That's too bad," she said. "My little brother Harry loves to swim!"

"I wish Stevie did," I said. "He seems to be afraid of everything. I never thought that having an adopted brother would be like this. He's only been here for three days. But already everything's changed. I don't like it."

"Can I see him?" asked Lynn. "Where is he?"

"Mom took him shopping with her," I explained.

Lynn settled back into the grass. "Well, thank heavens for summer vacation," she said, changing the subject. "Just think! Next fall we'll be in fifth grade!"

I nodded. "I'm going to be on the flag twirling team at school," I said. "Mom said she'd buy the uniform for me."

"Cool," said Lynn. "I'd give anything to be a flag twirler."

We lay back in the grass studying the

clouds above us in the blue Nebraska sky.

Lynn pointed. "That one looks like a castle," she said.

I peered carefully at the cloud. "It looks more like our dining room table with peas, carrots, and bread crumbs spilled all over it when Stevie gets done eating," I said.

Lynn giggled. She pointed at another cloud. "That one looks like a horse on a merry-go-round," she said.

I studied the white, puffy cloud. "I think it looks like the teddy bear Stevie ripped the ears and nose off," I said.

The cloud changed shape as winds blew high above us in the sky. "Now it looks like my favorite book that Stevie scribbled on with blue crayon," I added.

Lynn poked me with a blade of grass. "It can't be that bad, can it?" she asked.

"It's worse," I said. "When Mom and Dad told me we were adopting a four-year-old boy, I thought it would be great. I've always wanted to have a little brother. I figured I could teach him to roller-skate, climb trees, fly a kite, and skateboard. I was going to teach him to tie his shoes and do arithmetic, throw a baseball. But all he ever does is cry."

"What about?"

"Everything! The only thing that makes him stop crying is Mom singing to him. She says that probably his 'birth mother' sang to him."

"His 'birth mother'?" Lynn looked curious.

"That's the first mother," I explained. "The one who carried him inside her and gave birth to him. My mom is my 'birth mom.' Your mom is your 'birth mom.' Stevie's 'birth mom' placed him for adoption when he was a baby because she didn't have money to raise him, and because she wasn't married."

"That's sad," said Lynn.

"No one adopted him when he was a baby, so he grew up in foster homes," I explained. "People took care of him. But he didn't have a real mom or a real dad."

Star poked her nose into my face. I petted her. "Star doesn't like him either," I said. "He pulls her tail."

Lynn frowned. "Maybe all brothers are trouble," she said. "Harry isn't adopted, but he's still gross."

"He can't be as bad as Stevie is," I said. "Mom and Dad waited for a whole year to adopt him. And now that they have him, he acts like a jerk."

Lynn sat up and looked around. "Are you home alone?" she asked.

"No. Dad's fixing up Stevie's new bedroom," I said. "It used to be Mom's sewing room."

"Can I see it?" asked Lynn.

"Sure." We stood up and walked into the house with Star close behind. I heard my dad singing from Stevie's room.

"Tipi-yiyi-yay, come to the rodeo!" he sang.

Lynn looked curiously at me. I had to smile. "Dad sings cowboy songs when he works around the house," I said.

"But your dad's nothing like a cowboy. He's a lawyer," Lynn said.

I nodded and shrugged my shoulders. We

entered Stevie's room. The smell of new paint filled my nose. Dad sat on top of a ladder, pasting a strip of wallpaper along the top of the wall. A parade of blue ducks marched along the paper. There were ducks on the curtains and a duck on the lamp shade.

"Did we adopt a boy or a duck?" I whispered to Lynn. She began to giggle.

Dad turned around. "Hello, Lynn," he said. "Nice to see you."

"Hi, Mr. Towser," Lynn said.

Dad climbed down from the ladder. He had wallpaper paste on his nose. "What do you think?" he asked, waving a hand at the room.

I looked around. Stevie's new bed was against the wall. Plastic cars, blocks, puzzles, trucks, and stuffed animals were scattered across the floor.

"It's nice," said Lynn.

"It's a mess," I added. "Why does Stevie throw his toys all over the place? How can a little kid be such a slob?"

Dad grinned. "I remember a little girl who

used to make messes," he said.

"Who?" I asked.

Dad stared at me, grinning.

"Me?" I asked. "No way! I never made messes, at least not anything like this. I never threw things on the floor."

"Kelly's locker is always neat and clean at school," said Lynn, coming to my defense.

Dad threw back his head and laughed. "You used to throw your clothes all over the house when you were little," Dad said to me. His eyes twinkled. "You were four years old, Stevie's age. Sometimes your mother and I followed you around the house picking up clothes where you threw them. Sometimes you hid your clothes around the house when we weren't looking. Almost every day we found your clothes somewhere new."

I could hardly believe what I was hearing.

Dad scratched his chin, thinking back. "The first time you threw your clothes around, we found them on the television."

Dad turned to Lynn. "We even found Kelly's

underwear in the broom closet."

Lynn giggled.

It seems as if parents love to tell embarrassing stories about stuff their kids can't remember. "Are you sure it was me?" I asked.

"Sure I'm sure," said Dad. "You threw your underclothes all over the house. We began to call it 'the haunted underwear' because it turned up in the strangest places when we weren't looking!"

Lynn nudged an elbow into my side. I felt myself begin to blush.

Dad put his arm around my shoulders. "All little kids make messes, Kelly," he explained. "When you were little, we just made a joke out of it and called it the haunted underwear."

Dad looked around the room. Then he picked up a Nerf football from the mess of toys on the floor. "I think Stevie might grow up to be a great quarterback!" he said proudly. "He'll be just like I was back in college. My son, the football star!"

I frowned.

"Or maybe Stevie will be a cowboy," Dad said. "Tipi-yiyi-yi!" Dad sang. "Let's go down to the rodeo!" He was definitely in one of his happy moods.

I heard the front door open.

A voice squealed, "Let me have it! Let me have it!"

"Yuck!" I muttered. "It's Stevie."

"We're home!" Mom called out to us from the living room.

Star barked. Footsteps clattered down the hallway. Stevie burst into the room. "I got a new ball!" he said. "And new shoes. And a new eraser and new pencils!"

"I wish he had a new brain," I whispered to Lynn.

Stevie grinned from ear to ear, showing dimples in his cheeks. His black, curly hair sprang up from his head. Dark brown eyes sparkled.

Mom came into the room. "Hi, Lynn," she said. "Nice to see you."

Turning to me, she said, "Hi, sweetie." She

kissed me on the top of the head. Then she pulled Stevie's new clothes from a bag that she carried. "Aren't they cute?" she asked.

She held up a new, little T-shirt. It had a dinosaur on the front. There were dogs stitched onto the knees of his new pants. Ducks and alligators were on his sweatshirts.

"I got a new book, too!" Stevie shouted. He shoved the book in my face. It was about farm animals. There weren't many words on the pages. Mostly it just said "Moo-moo," "quack-quack," "oink-oink," and stuff like that.

Mom smiled at him. "Stevie," she said, "I want you to meet Kelly's friend, Lynn. She has a little brother, too. Harry is six years old. That's two years older than you."

"Does he have crayons and toys like mine?" Stevie asked. "Does he like to play with trucks? Does he have a mommy and a daddy?"

"Yes," said Lynn with a grin.

"This is my new mommy and daddy," said Stevie, pointing at my parents. Then he pointed at me and said, "You're my sister." Suddenly he

13

looked doubtful. "Are you really my daddy?" he asked, looking at my dad.

Dad nodded his head. "Yes, Stevie. I'm your daddy. You live here. This is your house. This is your room."

Stevie's chin trembled. Tears filled his eyes.

Dad's voice was gentle. "You're our son now. We'll always love you. We'll never leave you."

Stevie turned to my mom. "Are you really my mommy?" he asked.

"I sure am," Mom said, "and you're my little boy. We adopted you. That means that we'll always love you and take care of you."

I rolled my eyes. It seemed weird to hear my parents tell Stevie that they were his parents. After all, they'd always been my parents...for 10 years. But they'd only been Stevie's parents for *three days*.

Mom looked at the new wallpaper border. "Grant," said Mom, "the ducks really look wonderful!"

I turned just in time to see Stevie pull Star's tail. Star whirled around and barked. Stevie stepped backward and fell to the floor. His mouth opened wide, and he began to wail.

"Ow-w-wwwwwww!" he cried. "Star bit me!"

"She did not!" I said.

Stevie howled some more. Tears streamed down his cheeks. He ran to Mom. She lifted him up and held him as he sobbed on her shoulder. Mom began to sing softly to him. Dad turned to me. "Kelly, you'd better put Star in the backyard," he said. "But Dad," I insisted, "she didn't do anything." Dad's eyebrows lowered. "Kelly," he said, "put Star in the backyard. Stevie's afraid of her."

"But..." The look on Dad's face told me that I'd better not argue. I hooked my finger through Star's collar and pulled her from the room. She followed me down the hallway, her toenails tapping against the floor.

"See what I mean?" I said to Lynn, who walked beside me. "It's not the same around here. Stevie's ruined everything! My life will never be normal again...unless I can think of a plan to make things like they were before."

Two

THAT night, I lay in bed staring at the ceiling. It was hard to sleep because I could hear Mom in Stevie's room. She was singing him to sleep. I wished someone was sitting beside my bed, singing to me.

I stretched my arm into the darkness beside my bed, and felt Star lick my fingers "Good girl, Star," I said. It was nice to know that I wasn't alone as long as I had Star. I could always count on her to sleep beside my bed at night. I petted her head and whispered, "Good night."

I lay in the darkness, thinking about how it used to be before Stevie came...back when I was an "only" child...back when I had Mom and Dad to myself. It seemed as if they didn't have time for me anymore. I hoped things would change when the new school year began.

Maybe Mom and Dad will be proud of me when I'm a flag twirler at school, I thought to myself. *But school's a long way away. How can I ever make it through the summer with my new brother driving me nuts?*

* * * * *

Sounds outside my window woke me up Sunday morning. Yawning, I climbed out of bed, stepped over Star and looked out the window. There was Stevie with Dad. Dad held Stevie by the hands and was swinging him in a circle. Stevie's feet left the ground as Dad spun around. It was the same spinning game that Dad and I used to play every night in the yard when he came home from work. Only now he was playing it with Stevie. Stevie laughed and shrieked, just like I used to when Dad spun me around.

Quickly, I got dressed. Star followed me to the kitchen.

"Hello, sleepyhead," Mom said. She handed me a plate of pancakes.

"They smell great," I said. I set the plate on the table and headed toward the refrigerator to get the syrup bottle. Before I'd even taken three steps, I tripped over a plastic airplane on the floor. I caught myself at the last minute.

"I could have broken my neck!" I said. "Stevie shouldn't leave his toys all over the place. I always put my toys away. Stevie's the messiest kid I ever saw!"

Mom poured me a glass of orange juice. "You may not remember, Kelly," she said, "but you used to make messes, too. When you were little, just about Stevie's age, you would take your clothes and throw them—"

"I know, I know," I sighed. "Dad already told me about the haunted underwear. But I sure don't remember doing that."

Mom smiled. "Well, you did! You were too little to remember," she said. "It was the cutest thing! We'd find your underwear in the strangest places!"

I chewed a mouthful of pancakes. It seemed as if everyone remembered the stupid haunted underwear except me.

"Can Lynn come over today?" I asked. "We want to practice flag twirling. We're going to try out for the twirling team when school starts."

"Sure," said Mom. "Why don't you give her a call as soon as you're done eating?"

After breakfast I went to the phone. Just then Dad and Stevie came inside. "Get your Nerf football, Son," Dad said.

Stevie ran to his bedroom and returned with the football. He tossed it to Dad. Dad tossed it over the kitchen table. It bounced off of Stevie's stomach to the floor.

Boy! They always yelled if *I* threw things in the house!

Dad smiled at Mom. "He's a natural,

Sharon!" he said. "He'll be a great quarterback. I can tell. He'll be the star of the Neville Bobcat football team. Should we get him a little uniform?"

"Grant!" Mom exclaimed. "He's only four years old!"

"It's never too early to start practicing," Dad insisted. He looked proudly at Stevie. "I can see it now. My son, the football star!"

My son, the football star! Dad's words echoed in my head. I guess I never knew before how much he wanted a son, someone who could play football. It made me wonder if *I* should I go out for the school football team. Would Dad like me better as a quarterback instead of a flag twirler? Had Dad wanted a son all these years and not a daughter?

I heard something squeak. It was Star chewing on her rubber mouse. She did that when she wanted someone to pet her. I knew just how she felt. I patted Star's head and tickled her ears. She wagged her tail.

After Dad and Stevie went back outside, I called Lynn. She said she'd come over.

Star and I waited in the front yard for Lynn. I kicked off my sandals and wiggled my toes in the grass. Nearby, Dad was whirling Stevie around again. Stevie shrieked with excitement.

I glared at Stevie, then jumped up from the grass. "Swing me, too, Dad!" I exclaimed.

Dad looked at me kind of funny, but then said, "Sure, honey." He grabbed my wrists and swung me around in a circle, then another, and another. My toes kept nipping at the top of the grass, but my feet were off the ground. When Dad stopped, I staggered dizzily across the grass with Star barking and running circles around me. Then I fell on the ground. Star tugged at my T-shirt while I laughed.

"Whooh!" said Dad. He wiped sweat from his forehead. "Now I remember why we haven't done that in such a long time, Kelly. You've gotten too heavy for this game," he said.

"That wiped me out!"

I was about to tell him that we could always think of another game for just the two of us, but Stevie butted in before I could say a word.

"I want to go again!" he cried. "Swing *me*, Daddy!" Dad sighed, but he gave Stevie a long, whirling ride. He didn't say anything about Stevie being heavy.

I saw a dust cloud appear on the road in the distance. "Lynn's coming!" I said.

Her bike glittered in the sunlight as she came closer and closer. Star ran out to meet her, just as she always does.

"Hi, Star," I heard her say. Then she called out, "Hi, Kelly! Hi, Mr. Towser! Hi, Stevie!"

I watched my best friend guide her bicycle up the driveway. She put the kickstand down, then carefully lifted a brightly wrapped package from her basket. There was a blue bow on top

"This is for Stevie from my mother," she

said. She started to pass it to Dad.

"For me!" Stevie said. He grabbed the gift from Lynn. He tore at the paper and ribbon. "A dinosaur!" he shouted when he had ripped the paper off. "Yippee!" Stevie lifted the plastic dinosaur from its box. It was tall and green. He marched the dinosaur across the ground and onto my bare feet.

"The dinosaur is eating Kelly's toes," he announced. "Yum, yum." Stevie made pig eating noises as he pushed the dinosaur's head between my toes.

"Stop it!" I yelled, stepping backward.

Mom came out into the yard. "Hello, Lynn," she said. She looked at the dinosaur. "How nice! Thank you."

"My mom got it," Lynn said.

"Well, please tell her thank you for me, too," Mom said. "Stevie," Mom added, "why don't you put your dinosaur in your room. You don't want to lose it in the yard."

Stevie hugged the dinosaur to his chest. "Now I have a dinosaur, and a robot, and soldiers, and a teddy bear, and blocks, and a wagon, and lots of other toys!" he announced. With the dinosaur tucked under his arm, he ran into the house.

I stood there, frowning.

"What's the matter, Kelly?" Mom said.

"Everything!" I blurted. I didn't want to say anything with Lynn standing right there, but I couldn't help it. "Stevie gets *everything!*" I complained. "Dad painted his room and put wallpaper up. He has new bedroom furniture, and toys, and clothes, and books and presents. I'm not getting *anything*, and it's not fair."

Lynn didn't say a word. Mom and Dad looked at me, then at each other. Dad reached out and pulled me close. "Sorry, Kelly," he said. "We didn't mean to leave you out."

"That's right, honey," said Mom. She looked at me with a serious look. "I guess we haven't been paying enough attention to you. We've been so busy trying to make Stevie feel safe and loved in his new home."

Dad looked at me. "How do you like being a big sister?" he asked.

I was glad that finally someone wanted to know what I was thinking. "I'm trying to like it," I said honestly. "But I don't think Stevie should get everything. It's not fair."

"I'll tell you what," Dad said. He clapped his hands together. "Let's celebrate your new brother by buying you a gift, too. What do you want? Just name it."

I could hardly believe what I was hearing. Lynn's eyes grew wide with excitement.

"Can I think about it for a minute?" I asked.

Mom and Dad smiled. "Sure," they said at the same time.

I pulled Lynn off to a corner of the yard. "This is my big chance!" I said excitedly. "I could get new clothes or a basketball!"

"Or some video games!" suggested Lynn.

"Or a boom box!" I said.

"Or double-pierced ears and new jeans?" Lynn added.

"Or a membership to the zoo!" I said.

Suddenly, a black, wet nose pushed at my hand. Star dropped her toy mouse at my feet. I looked down into my dog's brown eyes. I patted her furry head. Then, all at once, I knew what I wanted.

"A puppy!" I exclaimed. "I want a new puppy!" "Bingo!" said Lynn, snapping her fingers. "That's the best idea of all!"

I ran back to Mom and Dad. Stevie had returned. He held Mom's hand. "I want a new puppy!" I said.

Mom and Dad didn't say anything. Dad frowned slightly.

I had to think fast. "Star needs someone to play with when I'm in school," I said. "Besides, there's room for her. We have a big yard."

Stevie jumped up and down. "I want a puppy! I want a puppy!" he yelled,

"You said I could choose something," I reminded them. "You said 'just name it.' Well, I choose a puppy."

Star wagged her tail. I could tell she thought it was a great idea, too.

Mom shrugged her shoulders. "We promised, Grant," she said.

"Okay, Kelly," said Dad, "we'll get a puppy. You can pick one out at the animal pound tomorrow."

"Cool!" said Lynn.

"Yay!" I said. "I'm getting a new puppy!"

"Yippeee!" Stevie shouted. "I'm getting a new puppy!"

The smile fell from my face. Turning to Stevie, I said, "This puppy is *mine!*"

"He's *mine!*" said Stevie.

Three

I was too excited to sleep that night. I wondered what the puppy would look like. Would he be brown or black or white, or all three? I wondered about Stevie, too. Would he ever be the kind of little brother I could like? Or would he always be the kind who pushes dinosaurs between my toes?

I reached down from the bed and felt for Star. I scratched behind one of her ears the way she likes. She pushed her nose into my hand. I couldn't see Star's eyes in the dark, but I bet they were wide open. And I bet she was thinking about the very same thing I was—new puppies to play with and little boys who pull tails.

* * * * *

The next morning was Monday, and Dad had to go to work. But Mom drove me and Stevie to the animal pound. It sounded as if a thousand dogs were barking in the building. A lady who worked there showed us where the dogs were. Each one was in a cage. Some dogs were big. Some were small. Some looked scruffy. Some looked brushed and silky. Most looked excited. All of them wagged their tails when they saw me.

"Can I have two puppies? Or three?" I asked Mom. "We've got room! Our yard's big enough! Can I have three puppies?" When I saw the look on her face, I didn't ask again.

Stevie poked his fingers through a cage door. "Get this one! Get this one!" he begged.

"Is that the one you want, Kelly?" Mom asked.

I shook my head. "No. I want to pick it out myself," I said.

"Get this one! Get this one!" begged Stevie.

I ignored him. I walked up and down the aisle. I wanted to take them all home with me. It was hard to choose only one. Then all of a sudden, I saw the best puppy of all. He was black and fluffy, with a white spot on his head. He jumped up and down, bouncing like a yo-yo. His little, pink tongue hung out. Brown puppy eyes sparkled.

I stuck my fingers between the cage bars. The puppy licked them. He barked and jumped.

"I think he likes me," I said.

"He likes me, too!" Stevie exclaimed.

The lady opened the cage and lifted the puppy out. I held him in my arms. He wiggled and squirmed. When I put him down, he rolled onto his back, showing his plump, pink puppy belly. Then he tried to climb my leg. When he wagged his tail, his whole body shook. I lifted him again.

"I think he loves me," I said.

"We found this puppy by the side of the road," the pound lady said. "He was a mess. He was covered with dirt. You could count his ribs. He was so hungry. Somebody left him. He didn't have a home." She shook her head sadly.

"How can people abandon their pets like that?" Mom asked with a frown.

"He's really cute," I said.

"Is this the one you want?" asked the lady.

I put my cheek against the puppy's silky head. His tongue flicked out and licked my nose. It was hard to imagine that anyone would leave a good puppy like this beside the road.

"I'll take him," I said.

"Let me have him!" begged Stevie. He reached up toward the puppy.

I held the puppy higher and close in my arms. He barked and squirmed. I think he knew he had a new family. And that I was

his new mom.

"You'll love your new home," I whispered to my new puppy.

"Let me have him!" Stevie whined.

I turned around so that I wouldn't have to listen to Stevie.

Mom paid for the puppy and signed some papers. Then we got to choose a dog collar from a big case.

"Get this one! Get this one!" Stevie insisted, pointing at a big, red collar.

I tried to ignore him. I chose a little, blue collar with silver bells all around it. I put the puppy on the floor, and Mom helped me put the new collar on him. It looked pretty against the puppy's black neck.

"What will you name the puppy?" asked Mom.

"Name him Boscoe!" shouted Stevie. He tugged on my arm, then tugged on Mom's shirt. "The puppy's name is Boscoe! I used to have a puppy named Boscoe!"

Nice try, I thought to myself. *But this*

isn't your puppy. He's mine!

The puppy ran around on the floor. He jumped on my leg. Each time he jumped, all the bells on his collar tinkled. It made me think of Christmas.

"I'll name him Jingle," I said.

"That's a nice name," Mom said.

"His name is Boscoe," Stevie insisted. He jumped up and down the way little kids always do when they're excited.

I tried to ignore him. I carried Jingle to the car.

"I want to sit in the backseat with Boscoe!" cried Stevie.

"*I'm* sitting in the backseat...with Jingle," I said.

Stevie's mouth opened wide. He began to cry loudly. He sounded like an ambulance siren.

Mom looked from Stevie to me. "He's *my* puppy," I reminded her. "You said I could have him."

I climbed into the backseat, holding Jingle

on my lap. It was only fair. After all, Stevie got everything else—dinosaurs, new bedroom wallpaper, Nerf balls, sweatshirts with animals on them, trucks, cars, and crayons.

Stevie cried even louder. I saw Mom's lips moving which meant she was counting to 10. She does that when she's trying not to yell.

Mom lifted Stevie into her arms. She held him close and sang a quiet little song into his ear. Finally, he quit crying. Mom got him into the front and latched his seat belt.

Turning his head, Stevie looked back at the puppy. "Hi, Boscoe," he said.

As we drove toward home, Jingle jumped all over me in the back. They don't make seatbelts for puppies. By the time we got home, there wasn't one inch of my face that hadn't been licked.

Mom hardly had the door open before Jingle ran into the house. We followed him. Star looked surprised—especially when Jingle nipped her tail. Jingle jumped up and nibbled Star's ears. The puppy was so short that he ran right underneath Star, through her legs.

Jingle loved Star's toys. He grabbed a plastic bone and chewed on it. Then he jumped on Star's rubber mouse and made it squeak. Star growled.

I shook my finger at Star. "You can share your toys," I said. "Jingle is just a little puppy. He likes to play."

I lifted Jingle up and gave him a hug. Then I put him down and went to the telephone. I called Lynn.

"Hi, Lynn," I said. "We got the puppy. I named him Jingle. Come over and see him! He's great!"

"I have to stay home and baby-sit," said Lynn. Her voice sounded sad. "I got stuck with my brother today. He's been awful!"

"What did he do?" I asked.

Lynn sighed. "He flushed my favorite seashell down the toilet. Then he flushed my Barbie wedding gown down the toilet. He tried to flush my new headband down the toilet, too, but I caught him."

"Gee," I said hopefully, "do you think *your* brother would flush *my* brother down the toilet?"

Lynn giggled.

Suddenly, I heard a yelp. Turning, I saw that Stevie was trying to pick Jingle up.

"Stop it!" I yelled at Stevie. "I have to go!" I said quickly to Lynn. I hung up and ran to Jingle's rescue. I pulled the puppy away from Stevie. "You're too little to hold him," I told Stevie. "You'll hurt him!"

Stevie's mouth opened wide. I got ready for the ambulance sound. Soon Stevie was wailing. Mom came into the room.

"Sh-sh-she w-w-won't l-l-let m-me hold Boscoe," sobbed Stevie.

Mom shook her head. "Kelly," she said, "can't you share the puppy?"

"He was hurting Bos...I mean, Jingle," I said angrily.

I picked Jingle up and ran with him to the front yard. We played together the rest of the day. Stevie came outside and hung around us, too. I watched him carefully so that he wouldn't hurt my new puppy. When Dad got home, I showed him what a great puppy I'd picked out.

When it was time for bed, Jingle followed me into the bathroom. I closed the door so that Stevie wouldn't bother us. While I brushed my teeth, Jingle licked my toes.

I said goodnight to Mom and Dad. Then I climbed into bed. Star curled up on the floor beside the bed as always. Suddenly, Jingle ran across the floor and jumped on Star as if she were a springboard. The puppy bounced up onto my bed. Star leaped up and began to bark.

"Mommy! Daddy! I'm afraid!" Stevie called from his bedroom.

A few seconds later, Mom stuck her head into my room. "What's going on in here?" she asked.

"It's just Star," I explained. "She's mad at Jingle."

Star was still barking, and now she was racing back and forth beside my bed. She kept looking at Jingle.

"Come on, Star," Mom said. "You'll sleep in the backyard tonight."

"Why can't she stay here?" I asked.

"Her barking frightens Stevie," Mom said.

Right then, Star began to bark louder.

"Mommy!" Stevie called from his room. "Make her stop barking! I'm afraid!"

"Come on, girl," said Mom. She took Star by the collar and led her out of the room. I heard Star's toenails clicking slowly down the hallway.

It seemed weird for Star not to sleep beside my bed. I was used to having her with me. She was always there during thunderstorms. She slept beside me when I was little, and when I used to think that monsters lived in my closet. She had slept in my room for 10 years, ever since I was a baby and she was a puppy. It felt strange to know that she wasn't there—and all because Stevie was afraid of a little barking.

"Mommy! Daddy!" Stevie yelled. "I'm afraid!"

My crybaby adopted brother was at it again. It seemed that he was always afraid of something.

Jingle snuggled close to me and licked my ear. The white spot on his head seemed to glow in the dark. I hugged my new puppy.

From the backyard came the sound of howling. Poor Star. She howled and howled. I knew just how she felt. She was probably wondering why we had to adopt a little boy who cried, threw things, and pulled tails. And maybe, like me, she was wondering if it were possible to un-adopt a little brother.

Four

THE next Sunday, our house was as busy as a bus station. A bunch of my parents' friends drove all the way from town to meet Stevie. They said things like "Congratulations on your new son!" and "We're so happy for you!"

Everyone brought presents for Stevie, too. There were so many new toys I could hardly see the floor in Stevie's room.

Star was penned in the backyard so that she wouldn't jump on the company. Lynn came over, and we sat in the front with Jingle. We watched people come and go.

Mrs. Perkins, a teacher from the school where Mom teaches, called to me. "Hello,

Kelly!" she said. "I see you have a new little brother. He's adorable! Those dimples! You're lucky! Every family should have a son and a daughter."

"They should?" I whispered to Lynn. "That's news to me. I always thought that my family did just fine without a son. I used to think that one daughter was enough. But maybe not." I sighed.

"There should be a law against little brothers," said Lynn in agreement.

Jingle jumped in the grass beside us. His collar jingled and jangled. "You silly pup!" I said. I gave him a big hug, wondering how anyone could ever leave a puppy by the side of the road.

"Jingle's lucky you saved him," Lynn said.

Our neighbor from down the road, Mrs. Craig, walked out of our house. "Stevie's so cute!" she said. "You must be awfully proud of your new little brother!"

I pretended as if I didn't hear her. "I'd be more proud of a pet rabbit," I whispered to Lynn. "How can I be proud of a little brother who cries all the time?"

I thought about Stevie with his dark eyes and black, curly hair. "He doesn't even look like us," I complained to Lynn. I pointed at my red hair and blue eyes. "Mom has red hair and blue eyes, too," I said. "And Dad's hair is brown, and his eyes are green. Stevie doesn't mix with our family. Just because Mom and Dad changed his last name to ours doesn't mean he's really a Towser."

"What did his name used to be?" asked Lynn.

"Adams. Stevie Adams."

Jingle and I played tug of war with a piece of rope.

"I don't understand why Mom and Dad like him so much," I said to Lynn. "He's nothing like I am. I'm neat. He throws his toys around. How can they like both of us when we're so different?"

"Remember, your Dad said you were a slob when you were little," Lynn reminded me. She giggled. "Don't forget the haunted underwear," she said. "That's a riot!"

"I don't remember doing it," I answered. I had to giggle a little. "They must have laughed when they found my underwear in the kitchen. I guess they thought I was cute and funny when I was little."

A familiar blue car pulled into the driveway. "Grandma! Grandpa!" I shouted. Jingle ran with me to see my grandparents. Grandpa climbed out of the car. He kissed me. "Hello, Kelly. How's Stevie?" he asked. "Did you know that your great-grandfather was named Steven?" He patted my head. "There's a long line of Stevens in our family."

"I didn't know that," I said.

Grandma gave me a squeeze and a hug. She held a package under her arm. It was wrapped in pretty paper with teddy bears all over it. I knew it was for Stevie. "Where's that new grandson of mine?" she asked.

"He's in the house," I said with a sigh. I pointed to Jingle. "This is my new pup.

He's your new grand-puppy."

Grandma and Grandpa laughed. Grandpa reached down into his pocket. "I brought a surprise," he said.

It wasn't really a surprise because Grandpa always brought a candy bar for me. "I'll share it with Lynn," I promised.

"Huh?" Grandpa looked confused. Then he pulled a toy soldier from his pocket. "Stevie will have another one to add to his collection," Grandpa said.

I could hardly believe that Grandpa forgot to bring me a candy bar. He had never forgotten before.

Grandma and Grandpa walked into the house to see my new brother.

Returning to Lynn, I said, "Everyone's forgetting that I even exist. I might as well be living on the moon. Maybe I should paint my face purple. No one would even notice."

"Maybe things will be normal after Stevie's been here for awhile," Lynn said.

"I doubt it," I said with a frown.

Jingle caught hold of my shoelace in his tiny puppy teeth. He pulled so hard that my shoe came off. Laughing, I chased him around the yard. I could hear Star barking at us from the backyard.

Finally, I grabbed my shoe away from Jingle. Mom called to me from the front door. "Kelly! Dinner's ready!"

Lynn hopped on her bike and pedaled off down the road to her home. I went inside with Jingle. I sat next to Grandpa and across from Stevie. It seemed as if Stevie's food went everywhere but in his mouth. He poked at his mashed potatoes with his finger. He picked up his pork chop in his hands.

Grandma smiled. "Here, Stevie," she said. "Let Grandma cut it up for you."

Stevie drank from his glass. Milk dribbled down his chin, spilling onto the table.

"Slow down, Son," Dad said. "Drink more slowly. Hold the cup with both hands."

Mom got up from the table. She walked toward the kitchen to get some paper towels to clean up the mess.

"Where are you going?" cried Stevie. He looked afraid, as if he thought Mom were going to disappear forever.

"I'm just going into the kitchen, honey," Mom said. "I'll be right back."

"Come back!" cried Stevie. He reached for Mom and knocked over the salt shaker.

"Oops," said Dad. "Careful, Son!"

Stevie's eyes filled with tears.

"That's okay," Mom said, returning from the kitchen. "No use crying over spilled salt!" She laughed. Stevie laughed along with her, his tears forgotten.

Grandma and Grandpa kept smiling at Stevie. "Did you get some nice new toys today?" asked Grandma.

"I got a robot doll and a rocket and blocks and crayons," Stevie announced. He pulled the little plastic soldier from his shirt pocket. "Look!" he said, proudly holding up the soldier. "Grandpa gave me this!"

"That's nice," I said. I wished it were my

birthday so that I could have lots of gifts. It didn't seem fair that Stevie got a thousand gifts and I didn't get anything—not even a candy bar. *Why is Stevie so special just because he's adopted?* I wondered.

Stevie took the soldier. He pushed him headfirst into his mashed potatoes. "Look!" Stevie squealed. "He's diving! Ker-pow!"

He made the soldier dance on his plate. A blob of potatoes covered the soldier's face.

Mom, Dad, Grandma, and Grandpa broke into laughter. Mom took the soldier away from Stevie. "Don't play with your food, honey," she said. Dad was laughing so hard that he had to put his fork down.

Just because parents are old, that doesn't always mean they're mature. It seemed as if my mom and dad liked babyish stuff. It was time to remind them of some of my own cute tricks.

"Remember when I was little?" I asked. "Did I really throw my clothes around the house? Wasn't I cute? Remember the haunted underwear?" I waited for my parents to start laughing at the memory.

But Stevie was the only one who laughed. "Haunted underwear?" he giggled. "Kelly has haunted underwear? Where is it?"

"That was a long time ago," I said.

"You were just about Stevie's age," Mom said. She leaned over to cut Stevie's meat.

Stevie, Stevie, Stevie, Stevie! Didn't anyone care about what I had to say?

From under the table, I felt a warm tongue lick my ankle. It was nice to know that someone still appreciated me. I dropped a piece of meat onto the floor for Jingle.

"Kelly!" Dad exclaimed. "Don't feed the dog from the table!" I jumped at his voice.

"Boscoe likes meat," said Stevie. "Don't put any mustard on it or he won't eat it."

"His name is Jingle," I said.

"He looks like Boscoe," said Stevie. Stevie reached for his cup. As he picked it up, some milk sloshed over the top onto the table. "Uh oh," he said. Dad winked at Mom.

51

"It looks as if someone needs some lessons in drinking from a cup," he said.

Stevie's eyes filled with tears. His chin trembled. It seemed as if the waterworks were about to begin again. Dad reached over and patted Stevie's shoulder. "It's all right, Son," he said. "We're not mad at you."

All Stevie had to do to get everyone's attention was spill a little milk. If it could work for him, it could work for me, couldn't it? I reached for my glass and knocked it over. A puddle of milk spread across the table. "Uh oh," I said.

"Kelly!" Mom exclaimed. "Run to the kitchen and get a towel. What's gotten into you? Where are your table manners?"

I felt my eyes fill with hot tears. I opened my mouth wide and was surprised to hear the howl that came out. It sounded a little bit like Stevie and a little bit like Star.

Grandma and Grandpa stared at me.

"Good heavens!" exclaimed Mom. "Don't cry, Kelly. You're too old for that. Just clean

up the mess!"

I ran to the kitchen for a towel. I couldn't figure it out. Mom sang to Stevie when he cried. But when I cried, she yelled at me. When Stevie spilled his milk, everyone felt sorry for him. When I spilled my milk, I had to clean it up. It was embarrassing for Mom to yell at me in front of Grandma and Grandpa. Stevie was only in our house for a few days, and already my parents were forgetting about me. It wasn't fair.

I felt like hiding in the kitchen. Star was lying on the floor. She thumped her tail when she saw me. "Good dog," I said, stepping over her to get the towel.

After dinner, my grandparents left. I went to my parent's bedroom with Jingle. I closed the door to make sure that my crybaby adopted brother didn't come in. I called Lynn on the telephone.

"Hi, Kelly," she said. "Is Stevie still driving you crazy?"

"He's worse than ever," I moaned into

the phone. Once I got started complaining, I couldn't stop! "I think my parents like little kids better than they like older kids. I've just got to do something to make them love me again. Stevie's always showing off. I just don't seem to matter anymore. Mom and Dad spend more time with Stevie than they do with me. I feel like the Queen of the Cooties. Everyone thinks Stevie's the cutest kid in the solar system!"

"Well, he is sort of cute," said Lynn.

"You wouldn't say that if you lived with him," I said sadly.

Jingle shook his head, making a sound like Christmas sleigh bells. He licked my hand and nibbled my fingers. I think he understood how I was feeling. Some dogs are smart like that.

Outside the door I heard a noise. It was probably Stevie trying to get in. As if he didn't have enough toys in his room to play with. Now he had to come and bother me!

"Go away!" I yelled. "Leave me alone!"

Tip-tap-tip-tap. It was the sound of Star's toenails tapping down the hall as she walked away. It wasn't Stevie after all. It was Star who had scratched at the door. She had known I was in here.

"Sorry, Star!" I called. I felt bad. "It seems as if nothing's going right," I told Lynn, "ever since Stevie came to live with us. It's not anything like I thought it would be."

"Maybe it'll get better," Lynn said.

I sighed into the telephone. "I don't get it," I told Lynn. "Everything was great before Stevie came. Maybe Mom and Dad wish I were a boy. I've got to do something...fast! Lynn, I'm going to win my parents back if it's the last thing I do!"

"What are you going to do?" Lynn asked.

"I've been thinking about it," I admitted, "and I've got a great plan to get my parents to like me again. My plan goes into action tomorrow! If this doesn't work, *nothing* will!"

Five

"ARE you sure this will work?" Lynn asked. She didn't sound too confident.

"Sure it will," I said. "I've been practicing all day. Look! There's the sign I made!" I pointed to the sign taped to our front door:

****

THE AMAZING DAREDEVIL
KELLY TOWSER
6:00 DRIVEWAY
BE THERE!!!

****

Lynn waited with me in the front yard.

57

My plan went into action as soon as Dad got home from work. When he saw the sign, he asked, "What's this all about?"

"It's a surprise," I said. "You'll see. Swing me, please, Daddy?"

Dad grabbed my hands and whirled me around in the air. My feet left the ground. It was just like old times. When he stopped, I stumbled dizzily across the grass.

"Where's Stevie?" asked Dad.

"He's in the house with Mom," I said. "Remember, be in the driveway at 6:00!"

"I'll be there," Dad said.

I played with Lynn, Star, and Jingle in the backyard.

"Six o'clock is show time," I whispered nervously to Lynn. "Mom and Dad will spend time with me for a change. They're about to discover how talented their daughter is."

"Why don't you do a flag routine?" asked Lynn. "They'd like that, wouldn't they?"

"Nah." I shook my head. "Dad likes football players better than flag twirlers. I've got to do something more exciting."

My puppy looked small next to Star. I found Star's favorite rubber mouse toy in the grass. Its head and tail were chewed off. The squeaker didn't work anymore.

"Jingle!" I said. "You're supposed to *play* with Star's toys, not *eat* them!"

I checked my watch. "It's almost 6:00! Show time! The brave, daredevil Kelly Towser will now amaze her family! I'll show Mom and Dad something to really be proud of!" I told Lynn. "No baby tricks for me! I don't have to cry like Stevie. I don't have to throw my haunted underwear around the house like I did when I was a baby. Not me. This act will knock their socks off!"

"Well, good luck," Lynn said. Even Star and Jingle looked excited.

I grabbed my bicycle and wheeled it through the gate to the driveway. My watch told me that it was 5 minutes past 6:00. "They're late!" I exclaimed.

With a sigh, I marched into the house.

"Mom! Dad!" I called. "It's past 6:00!"

I heard Dad in Stevie's room. Dad was singing his cowboy song, which he always sings when he's happy. "Tippy-yi-yi-yay!" sang Dad.

"Good boy, Stevie," I heard Mom say. "That's a nice house you built."

Then I heard a pile of blocks crash to the floor. "Mom! Dad!" I shouted. "It's show time!"

They appeared a moment later. Mom held Stevie by the hand. He was wearing green coveralls with frogs stitched over the knees. I wondered to myself if Mom and Dad would like me more if I wore clothes with turtles, giraffes, moo-cows, and ladybugs all over them. Would I have to start dressing like a baby?

"You're late," I said. Then I puffed out my bottom lip.

"Sorry, Kelly," said Dad. "I lost track of the time. What daredevil act do you have in store for us?" He grinned.

"Are you going to fly in a plane, Kelly?" asked Stevie. He seemed excited. "Are you going to ride an elephant? Will you jump out of a helicopter?"

"I'm fresh out of elephants and helicopters today," I said. It was just like my adopted brother to ask me silly questions.

Mom, Dad, and Stevie followed me outside. "Stand there by Lynn," I commanded. Lynn had her fingers crossed for me. Jingle chased Star in the grass beside the driveway.

"The great Kelly Towser will now perform a wonderful act!" I announced. "No one in Nebraska has ever done this before! Stand back!" I ordered. "This is a dangerous trick!"

"Dangerous?" asked Mom. "Kelly, what are you going to do? You're not going to hurt yourself, are you?"

"It's not part of the plan, Mom," I said. I grabbed my bicycle and began to ride in circles in the driveway behind Dad's parked car. First, I took one hand off of the handlebars.

"Careful, Kelly," said Dad.

"I wanna ride!" cried Stevie. "Let me!"

"No," said Mom. "You're too little. You'll learn how to ride a bike when you get older."

No baby tricks for me! I carefully took my other hand off of the handlebars, as I'd practiced. The bike began to wobble. But then it straightened out.

"Way to go, Kelly!" said Lynn. "Good trick!" Mom and Dad clapped their hands. Stevie clapped, too.

"Wow!" Stevie exclaimed. "I wish I could do that!"

I could tell that Stevie thought I was brave. Maybe he wasn't so hopeless after all. Maybe in a few years I would teach him how to ride a bike with no hands. After all, wasn't that what big sisters were for?

"That's quite a trick, Kelly," said Mom. "You really know how to handle that bicycle. But you'd better stop before you get hurt."

"Wait, Mom," I said. "There's one more part to the trick. Look!"

I put both hands back on the handlebars.

Then I stood up on the pedals. I stretched one leg out behind me. I felt as if I were flying. I glided down the driveway past Mom, Dad, Lynn, and Stevie. I turned gracefully by Dad's car.

Just then Stevie grabbed at Jingle. Jingle barked and scampered into the driveway—right into my path. When I swerved suddenly to avoid running over Jingle, I crashed into the back of Dad's car.

"Stevie!" I yelled. I fell onto the driveway with my bike on top of me.

"Kelly! Are you okay?" Mom shouted. She, Dad, Lynn, and Stevie ran over to where I lay in a heap on the driveway.

"You ruined my trick!" I yelled at Stevie.

"There's a big boo-boo on your knee," Stevie said. He pointed to a red, scraped patch on my knee. "There's a big boo-boo on your elbow, too. There's a giant boo-boo on your—"

"All right," I moaned. "I get the picture."

My whole body felt like one big boo-boo.

"Owwww!" I groaned. But I didn't want to act like a baby. So I jumped up from the ground as best I could. "It's just part of the act, folks," I said. "Nothing to worry about."

"If that was part of the act, I'm afraid to see the encore," said Dad.

"Kelly is a great flag twirler," Lynn said.

"Kelly," said Mom, "go in the house and wash those scrapes off. I don't want you doing that trick anymore. I think we've had enough daredevil acts for today."

"There's just one more," I said. "Please let me do just one more trick! I practiced it all day! Puhleeeez!"

"This next one won't ruin the paint job on my car, will it?" asked Dad. He was studying the back of his car where my bicycle crashed into it.

"No," I promised. "This is an animal trick, just like in the circus. Jingle and Star are part of this trick."

Stevie clapped his hands together. "Boscoe and Star! Yippeeeeeeee!" he howled. "Can we go to the circus?"

Before Mom and Dad could say anything, I called Star. She came to me, and Jingle followed her. I pulled a special leash from my back pocket and tied it around Star's collar.

"Star is a wild tiger!" I announced. "She likes to eat people for lunch—especially little boys who pull tails! If she escapes from her leash, she will eat your legs off!"

Stevie screamed and grabbed Mom's hand. "Don't let Star eat my legs!" he yelled. Mom lifted him up and held him in her arms.

I gave the leash a little tug, and Star began to run in a circle around me. I stood in the center of the circle, holding onto the leash. It was just like a real circus act.

"Come on, Jingle!" I called. "This is your part of the trick! Come on! Come on, boy!"

Jingle began to bark and dig in the ground. Dirt and grass flew into the air. That wasn't part of the trick.

"What's Boscoe doing?" asked Stevie.

"One of your tigers isn't behaving," said Dad with a smile.

"Your tiger is ruining the lawn," Mom said.

"Jingle's supposed to jump on Star's back," I explained. I was disappointed. Nothing was going right. "He did it this afternoon. He rode around on her back. Come on, Jingle! Come on, boy!"

Jingle quit digging. Then he ran closer. Suddenly, he jumped up on Star, just like we had practiced. Things were looking better!

But instead of riding on her back as he was supposed to, he bit her ear.

Star yelped and growled. She pulled away from me and rolled onto the ground, dragging the leash behind her. I fell onto the grass trying to grab her.

Dad ran over and caught Star. He looked at her closely. Then he untied the leash from her neck. "What is this?" he asked. He studied the leash, and suddenly I wished that I could jump on Star's back and ride away into the Nebraska sunset.

"Kelly, is this my tie?" Dad asked with a frown. "Is this my new tie?"

I hung my head. "I don't know," I said. "I mean, yes, it's a tie. But I don't know if it's new or not."

Mom inspected the tie. "That's the one I gave you for your birthday last month, isn't it, Grant?" she asked.

"The puppy chewed it," said Stevie. "It has dog slobber on it."

It seemed as if my career as a daredevil performer was coming to a fast end. First, I practically killed myself in the driveway, almost wrecking Dad's car. And now I was in trouble for getting dog slobber on his new tie. It was embarrassing to get in trouble in front of Lynn—but it seemed to be a regular thing nowadays.

"You're old enough to know better than this, Kelly," said Dad.

I stared at my feet. I wondered what "old enough" was. Was there some magical age when I wasn't supposed to get into trouble anymore? If you ask me, "old enough" was probably about 100 years old, not 10 years old like me.

"Come on," said Mom. "It's time for dinner." She started to set Stevie down on the ground.

"Hold me!" he screamed. "The tiger will eat my legs off!"

"Star is a dog, not a tiger," Mom said. "You silly thing." She kissed Stevie on the cheek and carried him into the house. Dad followed them into the house.

I viewed the scrapes, dirt, and grass stains on my legs and arms. A scab was beginning to form on my knee.

"I never knew the entertainment business could be so painful," I told Lynn. The scrapes were really starting to sting.

Lynn smiled. Star came over and licked my ear. Jingle tugged on my shoe lace. "Sometimes it seems as if the only people who really appreciate me are dogs," I said.

"I appreciate you," said Lynn.

"Thanks," I said. "I just wish my parents did, too."

Lynn hopped on her bike and pedaled off. I went into the house and sat at the table. I watched Mom cut Stevie's meat up for him. Dad wiped gelatin off of Stevie's chin with a napkin. Mom told Dad how Stevie played with toy cars and drew pictures that afternoon. She bragged about how Stevie could spell Nebraska.

Then Dad told me not to play with his ties anymore. And Mom said, "Keep both hands on the handlebars and both feet on the pedals, Kelly."

I glared across the table at Stevie. Everyone thought he was so cute just because his clothes had frogs and turtles on them.

What's the big deal about having an adopted brother? I asked myself. *He doesn't even look like us with his dark eyes and dark hair. Why did we have to get stuck with him? Why did Mom and Dad want to adopt a son? Wasn't I good enough for them?*

After dinner, I played with Jingle in the backyard. Then I took a bath. The "boo-boos" on my knees and arms stung in the hot water. Later, I crawled into bed with Jingle next to me. Star wasn't on the floor beside my bed. She had quit sleeping there ever since we got Stevie.

I knew Star wished it were like old times, just the two of us—before Stevie came to live with us. Dogs were smart like that.

Jingle snuggled against me. It felt good to have my new little puppy sleeping beside me. His wet tongue washed across my hand. That's a dog's way of kissing goodnight.

As I fell asleep, I wondered what I could do to get my parents to like me again. It seemed as if everything I tried—spilled milk, crying, daredevil tricks—didn't work. What could I do? I had to try something new.

Six

I jumped out of bed the next morning. The smell of pancakes filled my nose. Pancakes were my favorite breakfast! I ran to the kitchen. Dad sat at the table dressed for work. I noticed he was wearing an old tie. Stevie wore his pajamas with pictures of rabbits and foxes on them. He had a mouthful of pancakes and syrup. "Here comes Kelly!" he squealed. "It's Kelly the door-devil!"

"Daredevil," I corrected him.

Mom turned to me with a funny look on her face. I was surprised when she held up a pair of my underpants. "What are these?" she asked.

"Is this a trick question?" I asked. *Has Mom forgotten what girls' underwear looks like?* I wondered. "Uhh, they're underpants," I said.

"I know they're underpants," Mom explained. "But what are they doing in the kitchen? That's what I want to know."

I looked to Dad for a clue. I figured that this must be some kind of joke or riddle. "I don't know," I said. "What are my underpants doing in the kitchen?" I smiled and waited for the punch line.

Dad finished his coffee. "Kelly," he said, "underwear does not belong in the kitchen. Socks don't belong in the living room. T-shirts don't belong in the front hall."

"And goldfish don't belong in a hamster cage," I said, getting into the spirit of the game.

Dad frowned. Mom frowned, too. "Kelly, it was cute when you were four. But you're much too old to be throwing your clothes around the house."

"What?" I didn't understand.

"Can I have a hamster?" asked Stevie. "Can I have a goldfish?"

"I didn't throw my clothes around the house," I said.

Mom looked puzzled. "Your clothes were taken from the laundry basket upstairs. I found them scattered all around the house this morning. It's just like you used to do when you were little."

I looked at the pile of my underclothes that Mom held. "I didn't do it," I said again.

"You're not a baby anymore," Dad replied. "There are better ways to get our attention."

"I didn't do it," I insisted.

"Why is Kelly's underwear walking around the house?" asked Stevie.

"Maybe it's really haunted this time," I said with a hopeful grin.

"Does Kelly's underwear have a ghost in it?" asked Stevie.

I started to laugh. But Mom and Dad

just sighed. "Dirty clothes belong in the basket," Mom said. She handed me my clothes.

"I saw your underwear walking last night," said Stevie. "It floated in the air."

"Yeah, sure," I said. It was just my luck to get a new adopted brother with a wild imagination.

"I wish my underwear could fly like yours does," said Stevie. "Kelly, can you teach my underwear to fly?" he asked.

I wished that I could. Right then I wanted to teach Stevie's underwear to fly...to the moon...with Stevie in it!

I left the kitchen, returning my clothes to the laundry basket in the hallway upstairs. Downstairs I heard Stevie talking. Mom and Dad were laughing.

I felt so depressed that I called Lynn on the phone. Quietly, I told her, "It seems as if Mom and Dad don't even want me around anymore. I'm always in trouble lately."

I told Lynn about how Mom found my underwear downstairs.

"That's weird," Lynn said. "How did it get there?"

"It's a mystery to me," I said. "I mean, my underwear couldn't really be haunted, could it? But then how did it get thrown all over the house during the night? Who would do a thing like that? Why would someone want to get me into trouble with my parents?"

Suddenly a light went on in my head. I had my answer. There was only one person who wanted my parents to stop liking me.

"Stevie!" I whispered. "Stevie did it!"

Seven

THE next morning when I went to the breakfast table, the same thing happened. Mom handed me a pile of my clothes—underpants, T-shirts, and socks. "Kelly," she said, "underwear does not belong on the plants in the living room."

"I know that, Mom," I said.

Dad looked up at me from his coffee. "Young lady," he said, "we found your clothes scattered all over the house. The haunted underwear joke isn't as funny as it used to be. You're not a baby anymore."

"Kelly's underwear is haunted! Kelly's underwear is haunted!" cried Stevie. He waved his cereal spoon in the air. Corn flakes went sailing across the kitchen.

Mom cut a banana up to put on Stevie's cereal. Dad poured milk into Stevie's cup.

"I didn't do it!" I insisted.

Stevie looked up at me and grinned. I felt my temper rising.

My adopted brother is doing it! I wanted to shout. *He's the one who wants to turn Mom and Dad against me! It's not fair for me to be in trouble for something I didn't do. No one believes me,* I thought sadly.

After breakfast I went upstairs to my room and closed the door.

Jingle jumped up onto my bed and whined. He wanted a hug. I knew just how he felt. He cuddled up in my lap. I kissed him on the white spot on top of his head.

Squeals came from the backyard. I looked through my window. There was Stevie playing with Star. He kept throwing a stick. But Star didn't chase it. If Stevie had been friends with Star for as long as I had, he would have known that Star didn't chase sticks.

"He doesn't know anything," I whispered to Jingle. "He doesn't belong in this family!"

I took Jingle with me to the front yard. The grass tickled my legs as I sat down. My brain filled with thoughts about adopted brothers, underwear, and how I wished that my parents believed me.

Will the haunted underwear strike again tonight? I wondered.

* * * * *

When I woke up the next morning, I was almost afraid to get out of bed. I whispered into Jingle's ear, "I hope my underwear stayed in the laundry basket last night."

But as soon as I walked into the kitchen, I knew that the haunted underwear had struck again. Mom and Dad frowned at me. Stevie grinned. "The underwear ghost put your socks in the bathtub," he said. "Pee-youuuu! They stink!"

Dad held my socks in the air. Mom came

over and put her arm around me. In a gentle voice, she said, "Kelly, is there something you want to talk about? Is there a reason that you're doing this?"

Dad handed me the socks. "Kelly," he said, "we've asked you not to throw your clothes around the house. But you keep doing it. Is there something wrong?"

I pulled away from Mom. "I didn't do it!" I yelled. "Stop blaming me!" Pointing at my adopted brother, I shouted, "Stevie did it!"

Stevie's dark eyes grew round. His little chin began to tremble. That was always a sign that the waterworks were about to begin. It's a baby trick to get people to feel sorry for him. But it didn't work on me.

"Stevie's trying to get me in trouble!" I shouted.

Dad's eyebrows lowered. "Kelly!" he said. "I'm surprised at you! How can you blame your brother?"

"Stevie's not my brother!" I exclaimed. "He's adopted!"

Stevie began to cry. Tears poured down his cheeks. Mom picked him up and held him. Dad stood up from the kitchen table. "Young lady," he said, "go to your room."

I felt terrible. My parents were mad at me. They felt sorry for Stevie. But they didn't understand that he was lying. "He's the ghost!" I yelled. "He threw my underwear all over. Why don't you believe me?"

Sobbing, I ran to my bedroom with Jingle at my heels. I flopped onto the bed and buried my face in my pillow. Jingle jumped on the bed beside me. He licked my ear and whined. He knew something was wrong. Some dogs are smart like that.

I thought about Star penned in the back yard. I put my arm around Jingle. "You and Star are my only friends," I said. "Everyone else in this family hates me!"

I stifled my tears. "I won't be a crybaby like Stevie," I whispered. I heard the sound of Mom singing to Stevie. She always does that when he's crying. *Why doesn't she come in and sing to me? I wondered. Why can't it be like it used to be—just me, Mom and Dad? Why did they have to ruin everything by adopting Stevie? Our family was perfect before he came along.*

Then I had a terrible thought that made my stomach ache. *Do Mom and Dad love Stevie so much that they don't have any love left over for me?*

Mom's singing voice floated into my room. She was singing one of her favorite songs. "Hush little baby, don't say a word. Momma's gonna buy you a mockingbird."

I whispered to Jingle. "If Mom knew what Stevie was *really* like, she wouldn't think he was so cute." Jingle wagged his tail.

I sat up on the side of my bed. There wasn't any use in crying like a baby. I decided I had to do something. I went to my parents' room and dialed the telephone.

"Hello, Lynn?" I said. "You've got to help me think of a plan. I'm desperate!"

"What's wrong?" asked Lynn.

"It happened again," I said. "My under-wear flew all over the house last night... with a little help from my adopted brother. And now my parents are mad at me."

"Gee," said Lynn. "What can you do?"

"I've got to think of a plan," I whispered.

Suddenly, an idea popped into my head. "I'll catch him!" I exclaimed.

Holding Jingle in my lap, I said into the phone, "I know what I'll do. I'll stay awake all night and watch Stevie. I'll catch him tonight when he takes my clothes out of the basket. Then I'll have proof!"

"What will you do when you catch him?" asked Lynn.

"Uh, I'll worry about that later," I said.

"Are you sure this will work?" asked Lynn.

"It's got to!" I said. "At last I'll catch Stevie and solve the mystery of the haunted underwear. Mom and Dad will see they are wrong. Then they'll apologize to me."

My mind wandered away into a great daydream. In my daydream my parents apologized to me.

"We're sorry we didn't believe you, Kelly," they said. *"We should have known that you'd never lie to us. You're an honest and a wonderful girl! We feel terrible that we hurt you! Will you forgive us? Please?"*

"Are you still there?" asked Lynn.

"I'm here," I said. My daydream vanished. I whispered excitedly, "If this plan works, maybe Mom and Dad will realize what a great kid I am compared to Stevie. Maybe they'll feel so guilty for not believing me that they'll get me five more puppies from the pound! But first I have to catch the underwear ghost in the act!" I added.

I'd never stayed up all night before. Believe me, it's not an easy thing to do. When everyone else was in bed, I kept myself awake by thinking about how mad I was at Stevie. "He-stinks-he-stinks-he-stinks!" I chanted quietly to myself.

Moonlight came in through my bedroom window. As I climbed quietly out of bed,

Jingle jumped to the floor. His collar bells tinkled loudly. "Shhhh," I cautioned. Jingle whined softly as I closed the door and left him in my room. I had to leave him because puppies with jingle bells make too much noise when you're trying to catch a "ghost."

Star was lying in the hall outside my door. Her tail thumped happily on the floor when she saw me.

"Shh," I whispered again.

There was the laundry basket at the end of the dark hall. So far my dirty clothes were just where they should be—in the basket. Stepping past the basket, I tiptoed into Stevie's room. Carefully, I stepped over robots, plastic soldiers, blocks, teddy bears, crayons, a cowboy hat, and books.

In the moonlight, I saw Stevie asleep in the bunkbed that Mom and Dad bought for him. With his eyes closed and his mouth shut, he looked like a normal, nice, little boy. But I knew better.

Click-click-click. I heard the sound of Star's

toenails as she followed me into the room. She sat beside me in the shadows. I put my arm around her big, furry neck.

Stevie rolled over and muttered some words. I was relieved when he didn't wake up. He said something again, but I couldn't understand him.

Then Stevie pushed the covers off. His eyes fluttered open. He climbed out of bed. At last! The underwear ghost was about to strike! And I would catch him in the act.

I was afraid that Stevie would see me. But he didn't. He looked weird—sort of like the zombies in scary movies. He walked, but he didn't see me as I followed him.

"He's sleepwalking," I whispered to Star.

My heart began to pound. Was this the secret? Was he throwing laundry around in his sleep? At last I would catch the underwear ghost! When Stevie pulled my socks from the laundry basket I'd have proof!

I tiptoed behind Stevie. I was surprised when he walked right past the laundry basket.

Does he know I'm watching him? I wondered.

Star and I followed him downstairs into the living room. From there, we went into the kitchen. Then Stevie climbed back upstairs and went into his room. I couldn't figure it out. He didn't touch the laundry basket in the hall.

Stevie climbed into bed. He closed his eyes. Soon he was whispering in his sleep. I crawled closer and listened. I heard him say, "Please don't take me away, I want my mommy. Where's daddy? Give it to me. Please don't take me away. Come back!"

It sounded as if he was having a nightmare. He rolled in his bed. He made crying noises. Even in his sleep, he was a crybaby.

I yawned. It was time for me to go to bed. Star nuzzled my hand with her pointy, collie nose. It was her way of saying she loved me.

She followed me into my room. But she growled when she saw Jingle on my bed.

"Shh!" I warned her. "Don't wake Stevie

up. He'll cry. Then I'll get in trouble. I'm sorry my brother's such a wimp," I told Star. I gave her a goodnight hug. She lay down on the floor outside my room as I closed the door.

Jingle was glad to see me. He barked and jingled his collar. "Don't wake Mom and Dad up!" I warned him.

I crawled into bed, thinking about what I'd just seen. Stevie looked strange when he sleepwalked. He walked and talked. Yet he didn't seem to really see anything.

My eyes closed with sleepiness. I thought about my underwear in the laundry. *Maybe it really is haunted,* I told myself. *Maybe Stevie's not the one throwing my clothes around the house. But who else could it be?* A sudden thought flashed into my brain. Maybe *I'm* the one who's sleepwalking! Maybe *I'm* the underwear ghost! Could it really be *me??!!*

Eight

JINGLE jingled me awake the next morning when he jumped out of bed. It was like waking up to the sounds of Christmas. I pulled on my clothes and slipped my feet into sandals. Stevie's voice called from his room, "Mommy! Daddy! I can't tie my shoes!"

It seemed weird to hear him call my parents "mommy" and "daddy."

Jingle followed me from my room. We went to the kitchen where Dad and Mom were eating breakfast.

"What's for breakfast?" I asked. "Do we have any bananas left?"

Mom and Dad looked at me without saying a word. Suddenly I felt like a criminal on

91

that "America's 10 Most Wanted" TV show. "What did I do now?" I asked.

Mom held up a sock. Dad held up a T-shirt. It was the T-shirt with Batman on the front. It was definitely mine. "Where did those come from?" I asked weakly.

Dad didn't say a word. Mom sighed loudly. "Kelly," she said, "what am I going to do with you? I'm losing my patience."

I took the sock and the T-shirt. By now I could walk from the kitchen to the laundry basket upstairs with my eyes closed. In fact, I was beginning to wonder if I'd been doing just that. Was I sleepwalking? Or was it Stevie who was trying to get me into trouble after all? Had he sneaked out of bed after I was asleep? Or had *I* sneaked out of bed after I was asleep? Maybe Stevie wasn't the underwear ghost after all. Or maybe he was just a lot sneakier than I gave him credit for.

I dropped my clothes into the laundry basket. Peeping into Stevie's room, I saw him sitting on the floor. He pushed little cars along a track. "Beep! Beep!" he said.

"Hi, Kelly!" he said when he saw me standing in the doorway. "Want to play? I'm playing jungle! You can be the giraffe, and I'll be the monkey."

He was so cute that I had to laugh. Four-year-olds can be funny—when they're not driving you crazy! "How do you play?" I asked.

"My room is the jungle. This is the bad, old bear, and he's trying to get us," explained Stevie. He held a smiling teddy bear.

"Grrrr-r-rrrrr!" Stevie growled. He chased himself with the teddy bear. "Help! Help! Don't eat me, Mr. Bear!" Stevie shrieked. "I'm just a little monkey! Eat the giraffe instead."

Stevie held the teddy bear in my face. "You're supposed to run away," he informed me. "You're the giraffe. The bear wants to have you for lunch."

"Okay," I said. It was a silly game. But

it didn't hurt to play along. I ran across Stevie's room. He chased me around the room with the teddy bear.

"Grrrrrrrrrr!" he roared. "I'm a bear!"

"I thought you were a monkey," I said teasing him.

Stevie frowned. "I'm a bear *and* I'm a monkey," he explained.

"I'm a giraffe and I'm a dump truck," I joked. "Honk! Honk! I'm going to run over the bear." I walked toward Stevie.

"You can't be a truck! You're a giraffe!" Stevie yelled. He stomped his foot on the ground. His face turned red. "Get out of my jungle!" Stevie threw the teddy bear at me. It bounced off my arm. He began to cry. He sounded like an ambulance siren again.

Geez, what did I do? I asked myself as I left Stevie's room and returned to mine. I had to admit that he was cute sometimes. But he sure couldn't take a joke. I wished that he wasn't such a crybaby. And I wished that he wasn't trying to get me into trouble with my parents by throwing my clothes around the house.

But then I reminded myself that it might not be Stevie after all. Maybe it was me! Was I the underwear ghost? Was I playing tricks on myself in my sleep?

There was only one way to find out. "I'll set a trap for myself," I whispered.

That night I said goodnight to Mom and Dad. Then Jingle and I went to my bedroom. I closed the door and stuck a piece of tape from the door to the wall. I explained to Jingle, "If I open the door in my sleep, the tape will pull away from the wall. I'll check it in the morning when I wake up. Then I'll know if I'm sleepwalking."

Jingle ran and jumped onto my bed. I slipped underneath the covers.

I heard Stevie call from his room, "Mommy! Daddy! I'm afraid! Don't leave me!"

Mom and Dad rushed to Stevie's room. I heard Mom sing quietly to Stevie. I knew that she was probably holding him. I wished that Mom would hold me and sing to me. Even if I'm not a baby, it's nice to be held.

I lay in the darkness thinking about Stevie and how he was so afraid to be alone. "Jingle," I whispered, "it seems as if he always has to have Mom or Dad with him. He spends more time with them than I do—and they aren't even his real parents."

At last I heard Mom and Dad leave Stevie's room. They went to their bedroom. That meant that Stevie was asleep—or that he was *pretending* to be asleep.

I stayed awake as long as I could, listening for sounds of the underwear ghost. But no one walked in the hallway. As I was falling asleep, I wondered if I would soon be sleepwalking all over the house, throwing my socks around like boomerangs.

I woke up pretty early on Saturday morning. I couldn't get back to sleep because I had so much on my mind. Holding my breath, I checked the tape on my door.

"It's still there, Jingle," I said with relief.

"That means that I didn't open it last night. I'm not sleepwalking." Jingle barked. "Shh!" I told him. "Don't wake anyone up."

I opened the door. Star was sleeping on the hall floor outside my door. She wagged her tail when she saw me. After a quick pat on her head, I stepped past her. I tiptoed down the hall and down the stairs with Jingle behind me.

I found what I was looking for in the living room. There was my T-shirt...in the magazine rack. My socks were in the nut bowl on the coffee table. Quickly, I picked my clothes up. I found underpants and shorts under the kitchen table.

"This is getting ridiculous," I muttered, starting to get mad again. The tape trick showed me that I wasn't sleepwalking. I hadn't left my room the night before. So it had to be someone else throwing my clothes around. And the only person it could be was my little, crybaby, adopted brother. "This proves it!" I exclaimed.

I ran upstairs and put my clothes back in the laundry basket. Star was still in the hallway. Her tail thumped against the floor when she saw me. But her tail quit thumping when she saw Jingle.

Suddenly I heard, "Mommy! Where are you?" It was Stevie calling from his room. "Mommy, don't leave me!" he cried.

Mom came out of her room, pulling her robe on. "Good morning, Kelly," she said. "You're up early!" Then she hurried past me into Stevie's room. "Here I am!" she said.

"Mommy! Mommy!" Stevie squealed when he saw her.

"Mommy, Mommy," I growled under my breath.

It felt great to eat breakfast without everyone yelling at me. It was a good idea to put my clothes in the laundry basket before anyone got up. Mom stirred fresh orange juice in a pitcher. It would have been just about perfect if Stevie hadn't been there.

Dad walked into the kitchen. "I think that this family needs to spend some time together," he announced. "Are you in the mood for a picnic?"

"Yippeee!" I shouted. "Let's go!"

Dad grinned. "We can pack a lunch and go to Pinehill Woods."

Mom smiled. "I'll make some sandwiches," she said.

"I wanna go! I wanna go!" Stevie wailed. His chin began to quiver. "Let me go, too!" he pleaded.

Dad gave him a hug. "Don't worry. You're coming, Son," he said.

"You won't leave me home?" Stevie asked.

"No, we won't leave you," Dad answered.

It looked as if my adopted brother was having another attack of chicken nerves.

* * * * *

We had a great time at Pinehill Woods. Dad brought a Frisbee disk. We threw it around. Star caught it in the air and brought it back to us. But whenever Jingle got it, he ran away with it and we had to chase him. By the end of the day the disk had lots of little dog teeth holes in it.

It was dark by the time we got home that evening. Stevie had his bath first. Then I had mine. I was so tired that I fell asleep five minutes after I got into bed.

I woke up Sunday morning to the sound of rain drops on my window. Jingle and I climbed out of bed and went to the kitchen. There was Mom standing with my underpants and socks in her hands.

"Oh, no!" I groaned. "Not again!"

Nine

"THE underwear ghost came last night!" shouted Stevie.

Some families are visited by the Tooth Fairy, Santa Claus, or the Easter Bunny. But not us. We get the Underwear Ghost.

Dad sat at the kitchen table in his weekend clothes. I wished that it were a work day and that he weren't home so that he wouldn't be mad at me.

Dad frowned. "Kelly," he said, "this has gone on long enough. You're losing your TV privileges for two days."

"No TV?" I exclaimed. "I didn't do it!"

Mom shook her head. "This has to stop, Kelly," she warned, "no TV until Tuesday."

There wasn't any point in arguing with them, even though I was boiling on the inside. They didn't believe me and it wasn't fair. I just took my clothes and put them back in the basket upstairs. Jingle scampered up the steps behind me.

With a sigh, I said to the puppy, "I guess I'll have to get up early every morning. Then I'll pick my clothes up before Mom and Dad see them. But I'll never get enough sleep."

Jingle barked. I think he understood me.

"That's right, boy," I said patting his head. "Mom and Dad will apologize to me as soon as I prove that it's Stevie who is pulling the underwear trick. I'll be the favorite kid again."

I was more determined than ever to catch the underwear ghost. That night I stayed awake by reading scary stories under my blanket with a flashlight. The stories kept me awake. But they also made me afraid to get out of bed. Still, it was the only way I could keep myself awake so that I could catch the underwear ghost.

After I finished reading "The Green, Headless, Bloodsucking Monster," I stepped onto the floor beside my bed. I had a feeling that a green, headless, bloodsucking monster might be lurking under my bed. But I pushed thoughts of monsters, witches, ghosts, and haunted houses from my mind. Soon all I could think about was my adopted brother and what a pain he was.

Jingle followed me to the bedroom door. His collar made jingly noises in the dark. "No, boy," I whispered. "You stay here."

Jingle whined.

"Shh!" I answered.

I opened the door and slipped out into the dark, silent hall. Star's tail thumped against the floor when she saw me. Jumping to her feet, she followed me into Stevie's room. I think she liked my midnight visits.

It wasn't long before Stevie began to mutter in his sleep. He climbed out of bed and began his zombie-walk through the house. Star and I followed him down the hall, past the laundry basket, and down the stairs. But all he did was walk around the house. Then he came back upstairs.

I was hoping that he would grab some of my clothes, and then the mystery would be solved at last. But Stevie passed by the laundry basket and went back to his room. He climbed into his bed and began to talk in his sleep.

"Don't leave me," he cried. "Come home! Take me too! It's mine! Give it to me!"

He rolled around in bed. It sure sounded like he was having a nightmare. I sat, listening, until very late at night. It was kind of creepy. Star lay curled up at my feet.

At last I began to feel sleepy and I went back to my room. I closed the door, leaving Star out in the hall.

It seemed as if I only slept for about five minutes. Then it was morning. The sound of my family walking around woke me up. I got dressed, and Jingle and I went down to the kitchen.

I could hardly believe what I saw when I got there! A pile of my underwear sat on the kitchen table. Mom opened her mouth.

"I know," I said. "Underwear does not belong in the kitchen."

"You're supposed to wear your underwear under your clothes," Stevie informed me. "Even babies know that."

I rolled my eyes at my adopted brother. I felt like yelling at him, but I didn't. I was glad Dad had already left for work. I'd rather have one parent mad at me than two.

"Kelly, you've got to stop behaving so childishly. You may not watch any TV for four days," Mom said. "The TV's off limits until Saturday."

"But, Mom..."

"Don't argue with me, Kelly."

It wasn't fair. But what could I do?

* * * * *

That night, Star and I stayed in Stevie's

room all night long. We watched as Stevie sleepwalked through the house. But he didn't touch the clothes in the laundry basket. The sun was coming up when I slipped back to my bedroom for a few hours of sleep. Star stayed outside, as usual.

That morning, Mom was waiting in the kitchen with a platter of waffles, a plate of bacon, and a stack of my underwear.

I returned my underwear to the basket and called Lynn on the telephone. "I'm beginning to wonder if my underwear really is haunted," I told her.

"Kelly, you're kidding," she said. "Underwear doesn't just get up and walk around. At least not without people in it."

"I'm not so sure," I sighed. "Star and I stayed in Stevie's room all night long. How could Stevie get out of bed without us catching him?"

"I don't know," Lynn answered. "Maybe you fell asleep for a short time but didn't know it. He might have gotten up then."

"Maybe I'm going crazy," I admitted. "Maybe having an adopted brother has turned my brain to Jello."

That afternoon I found Mom planting flowers in the front yard. Stevie was inside taking a nap. I was the one who needed a nap! It seemed like a miracle to be with Mom alone. It was great to have her all to myself. She smiled at me.

"What do you think of your new brother?" she asked. "Is there anything you want to talk about?"

I was glad she finally asked me what I was thinking. "Yes, Mom," I said, taking a deep breath. "There's some stuff I think you should know."

Mom wiped dirt from her knees. "I'm listening," she said.

"Stevie has nightmares every night," I said. "He cries in his sleep. He's always afraid to be alone. He sleepwalks all over the house. I've seen him do it. I think there's something wrong with him."

"He's sleepwalking?" Mom asked. "He has nightmares?" She sighed and sat back in the grass. "I guess I'm not surprised," she went on. "Children sometimes walk in their sleep and have nightmares when they feel afraid. Some adopted children are frightened when they move into a new home. Sometimes adopted children have special needs."

"Special needs?" I didn't know what she was talking about. Stevie looked like a normal kid to me.

"Kelly, let me tell you something about Stevie," Mom said. "You know Stevie's mother placed him for adoption when he was two years old. She just couldn't take care of him anymore. She had no money and she wasn't married. So she thought it would be best for Stevie if he was in a home with a mother and a father."

"Yeah, I know."

"Stevie's lived in different foster homes for the past two years. Foster families took care of him. But they didn't adopt him. No one knows where Stevie's father is."

"Well, why does he cry all the time?" I asked. "He's afraid of *everything!*"

Mom smiled. "What Stevie's really afraid of is that he'll never have a real home," she explained. "He's afraid that no family will ever keep him. He's been moved around so much. That's why he's afraid to be alone. That's why he cries whenever I go somewhere. He's afraid I won't come back."

"Where's Stevie's real mom now?" I asked.

My mother looked at me. "I'm his real mom," she said gently. "Now that he's legally adopted, he's my *real* son. He's your *real* brother. I don't know where his 'birth mom' is. Kelly, we have what's called a 'closed adoption.' That means that we don't know the name of Stevie's birth mom. She doesn't know our name either."

Just then, I heard whining and scratching from the front door. It was Jingle wanting to be let outside. He pushed at the screen door until it opened. Then he ran outside.

He was so happy to see me that he jumped on me and licked my face. It was hard to believe that this wonderful puppy was ever left by the side of a road. Why would anyone ever give such a wonderful pup away?

Suddenly, I had an idea. "Mom?" I asked. "Is Stevie sort of like Jingle? They both need lots of care, right?"

Mom smiled. She reached out and squeezed my hand.

"That's right, Kelly," she said. "You 'adopted' Jingle so you could love him and care for him. We adopted Stevie so that we could love him and take care of him, too."

I thought about it for a minute. I did feel sorry that Stevie didn't have a home until he came to live with us. I was sorry that his birth mom couldn't take care of him. I was sorry that his *real*...I mean his *birth* father didn't want him.

I felt as if I should love him. But it was hard to love someone who was always trying to get me into trouble.

"Kelly, I want you to know that you can always talk to us about Stevie and about adoption," Mom said. "Is there anything else on your mind?" she asked. Mom pulled her gardening gloves on.

I wanted to tell her about how Stevie was the one who was playing the haunted underwear trick. I wanted her to know how he was trying to push me out of the family. But I knew she wouldn't believe me. But once I had proof, Mom and Dad would understand why I couldn't love my adopted brother the way they wanted me to.

"Come on, Jingle," I said. My puppy followed me out into the yard where we rolled together in the grass.

I whispered into Jingle's ear. "Tonight's the night. I'll stay up all night long. I won't sleep even for a minute. I'm going to catch the underwear ghost tonight. At last Mom and Dad will know who's causing the problems in this family!"

Ten

I tried to stay awake the best I could that night. But I had missed so much sleep the few nights before that I just couldn't. I fell asleep dreaming about giant turtles stealing my underwear. It was late, around midnight, when suddenly I woke up.

"Jingle?" I whispered. But the puppy wasn't lying beside me in bed. His collar bells tinkled somewhere in the darkness. Then I heard him whining and scratching at my bedroom door, trying to get out.

"What's the matter, boy?" I asked. "What's wrong?" Then I heard it. There was definitely a sound in the hall outside my door. Was it the underwear ghost? Was I going to catch him in the act at last?

I sat straight up in bed, listening. It was a weird feeling knowing something was going on outside my door. I could hear it. My heart started to race faster as I thought about Stevie. He was out there sneaking around...pulling my clothes out of the laundry basket...scattering them around the house...tiptoeing back to bed...just waiting for Mom and Dad to get up in the morning and yell at me!

Why was he doing it? "He wants to be the favorite kid," I whispered to myself. "He doesn't want Mom and Dad to love me anymore."

Even though I felt sorry for Stevie because he'd been passed around from family to family, I felt myself getting angrier.

It's not fair that I have a new brother who doesn't like me, I thought to myself. *He doesn't want to be my friend. I wanted a little brother to fly kites with, to roller-skate with, to walk to school with. Instead, I have a little brother who cries all the time, who's afraid to be alone, and who can't keep his hands off the dirty laundry.*

Suddenly, I heard something slide down the hallway. Was it the sound of a little boy's feet in slippers?

Jingle whined. "Be quiet!" I hissed. I climbed out of bed. In the darkness, I tiptoed across the room and put my hand on the doorknob. Turning it as quietly as I could, I pulled the door slowly open.

The hall was dark and shadowy. There was just a little light from the moon shining in the hall window. At first I couldn't see anything. But then I saw something that made me hold my breath.

Something moved at the top of the stairs.

It was one of my T-shirts being dragged along the floor. I watched as it disappeared beyond the landing and down the stairs.

At last! The underwear ghost wouldn't get away from me this time! Finally I was about to solve the mystery of the haunted

underwear! Mom and Dad would have to believe me now that I had proof, now that I was about to catch Stevie red-handed! I tiptoed slowly along the hall. I got ready to stop him in the act.

Then I heard Stevie call, "Mommy! Don't leave me! I'm afraid!"

But his voice was coming from his bedroom, from behind me.

Eleven

STEVIE was having another nightmare. But how could he be in his room having a bad dream and walking downstairs at the same time? My skin froze with goosebumps.

Who just disappeared over the top of the stairs? I asked myself. *Who's dragging my clothes around the house?*

Taking a deep gulp, I crept to the stairs. I stared down into the shadows and saw the end of my T-shirt disappear around a corner. Whoever had my clothes had gone into the living room. The sound of Jingle's bells gave me courage. I patted the puppy. The white spot on his head seemed to glow like a night light.

Slowly, I tiptoed down the stairs with Jingle

behind me. Something was moving in the living room. Carefully, I stuck my head around the corner wall. As my eyes adjusted to the shadows, I could hardly believe what I saw!

"It's you!" I cried.

There was Star with my T-shirt in her mouth. She dragged the T-shirt across the floor, then dropped it onto the coffee table. She pawed at a sock, scooting it under a chair.

Star wagged her tail when she saw me. But her tail quit wagging as soon as she saw Jingle. She walked past us as if her feelings were hurt.

I followed her up the stairs. She walked to the laundry basket and stuck her nose into the clothes and rooted around. Then she pulled out my underpants and held them in her teeth.

"Star!" I exclaimed. "You're the underwear ghost!"

Jingle scampered over to Star. He grabbed the other end of my underwear. They pulled as if they were playing tug-of-war. Star growled. Then I heard *R-r-r-rrrrip!* Each dog held a scrap as my underwear tore into two pieces.

Jingle rolled on the floor, trying to get Star to wrestle. But Star came over and dropped the torn underwear at my feet. That's the same thing she used to do with her rubber mouse...before Jingle chewed its head off.

"What's the matter, girl?" I asked, patting the collie's head.

She wagged her tail.

I stared into Star's brown doggie eyes. "Why did you do it?" I asked. "Why did you get my clothes out of the laundry?"

Star licked my hand. Jingle ran up and nipped Star on the back leg. She turned and growled. Then Star licked my hand again, wagging her tail.

Suddenly, I understood everything. After all, Star was my oldest friend. When you've been friends as long as we have, you begin to understand each other. I slipped my arm around Star's neck and gave her a hug. She was part of the family long before Jingle was.

"I'm sorry, girl," I said. "I've been ignoring you. I didn't mean to."

I watched Jingle somersault across the hall, chasing his tail. I giggled. Puppies are funny no matter what they do. And Jingle, with the white spot on his head, seemed to me to be the cutest puppy in the world.

But Star, my old dog friend, needed me, too. I'd had so much fun playing with my new puppy that I'd forgotten my old friend. We didn't even sleep in the same room anymore since Jingle came to live with us.

"Is that why you dragged my clothes all over the house?" I asked. "Were you trying to tell me something?" Star wagged her tail.

Jingle barked. His bells jangled as he chased his tail. "Be quiet!" I whispered.

The hall light flashed on. "What's going on?" asked Dad. Mom stood behind him.

"What are you doing playing with the dogs at this time of night?" asked Mom.

"Look!" I said, pointing at Star. A scrap of my underwear lay at Star's feet.

"What's Star doing with your underpants?" asked Mom.

"Don't you get it? She's the underwear ghost!" I said. "It was Star all along. She was jealous of Jingle. She missed me! So she tried to get my attention by dragging my clothes around." I gave Star another hug as she sat beside me. She thumped her tail on the floor.

My parents looked from Star to the laundry basket to me. "Oh, honey," said Mom. "I thought you were just trying to get attention."

"I was," I admitted, "but Star was, too. The underwear was *her* idea!"

Dad said, "I thought you were pulling the haunted underwear trick again. I should have believed you. I'm sorry, Kelly. I was wrong."

It felt great to know that my parents believed me...at last. But they weren't the only ones who needed to apologize.

"I was wrong, too," I said. "I shouldn't have blamed Stevie. I thought he was trying to make you...not love me anymore." I felt a lump rise in my throat.

Mom and Dad looked surprised. "Not love you anymore?" Mom asked. She knelt on her knees and kissed me.

Dad lifted me up into his arms, the same way he lifted Stevie. "You're our special girl, Kelly," he said. "You always will be. Our love for you never changes, no matter what happens."

I felt tears in my eyes. Suddenly I felt like the crybaby in the family. "Really?" I asked. "You don't wish I were a boy, or a football player? You don't wish I were four years old? You don't wish I wore clothes with frogs and skunks and ducks on them?"

Dad laughed and held me closer. "We love you just the way you are," he said.

"That's right," said Mom. "No matter how big you get, you'll always be our special girl."

I breathed a sigh of relief. Then I heard a cry from Stevie's room. "Mommy!" he called. "Don't leave me alone! I'm afraid! No! Come back!"

"Stevie's having a nightmare," I explained.

Mom began to walk down the hall. "I'll go sing to him," she said. "That calms him down."

I grabbed Mom's robe. "Wait!" I cried. Mom looked surprised.

"Let me go with you," I said. "I'll sing to him. After all, he's my brother."

I sang to Stevie about how some day we would fly kites together, and pick strawberries, and do somersaults together in the grass. I sang to him about how I would teach him to climb trees. I made up the tune and the words. They didn't rhyme. But he didn't seem to care. At last he fell into a peaceful sleep. I said good night to Mom even though it was morning. Then I went back to my room.

I lay there for a while, but I couldn't sleep. There were so many thoughts and feelings going around inside me. I wanted to talk to someone. So I went down into the kitchen and called Lynn, even though it was early in the morning. I knew she wouldn't mind.

"Hello?" Her voice sounded sleepy.

"Hi, Lynn," I said. "I caught the ghost!"

"You did? Did Stevie get in trouble?"

"It was Star!" I exclaimed.

"What? The ghost was a dog? Are you kidding?" Lynn asked.

"Nope," I said. "After I caught her it made me wonder. Did you ever stop to think that maybe people are like dogs?"

"Kelly, are you crazy?" asked Lynn.

I laughed. "No," I said. "It's just that I think people and dogs are alike sometimes. I'm sort of like Star. She needs lots of love, and so do I!"

"Jingle needs love, too," Lynn reminded me. "Maybe people are sort of like dogs," she admitted.

"I love Star and I love Jingle, too," I said. "I could probably love a million dogs if Mom and Dad would let me have that many!"

"A million dogs? Your house would smell terrible," Lynn said.

"I've been thinking," I said. "I love *both* my dogs. And Mom and Dad love both me and Stevie. I was afraid that they didn't love me anymore. But I guess your heart doesn't get crowded when you love more than one person. It just gets bigger!"

"Hmmmmm," said Lynn. "Can someone feel her heart getting bigger?"

"I'm not sure," I said.

I stopped to see if I could feel my heart growing with love. It didn't feel any different.

I said, "I think there's room in there for you, Mom, Dad, Star, Jingle—and Stevie." I thought about it for a moment. Then I added, "There's some room left over."

"There is?" Lynn asked. "For who?"

"Well," I said, "my heart's big enough for a parakeet, a pony, three kittens, four goldfish, a turtle, and some white mice."

Lynn giggled. "It sounds as if your heart is getting gigantic," she said. "Any room left over?" she asked.

"Yeah," I admitted.

"Room for who?" asked Lynn.

I smiled into the telephone. "There's room for another little brother or sister someday," I said. "Maybe Mom and Dad will adopt again."

"Would you like that?" asked Lynn.

"You bet I would!" I exclaimed. "I just hope the next one is as cute as my brother Stevie!"